W9-BRF-151

My Book
by Jane Belk Moncure
illustrated by Vera Gohman
THE CHILD'S WORLD
ELGIN, ILLINOIS 60120

Library of Congress Cataloging in Publication Data

Moncure, Jane Belk.
My "i" book.

(My first steps to reading)
Rev. ed. of: My "i" sound box. © 1984.
Summary: Little "i" fills her box with inchworms and other things beginning with the short letter "i."
1. Children's stories, American. [1. Alphabet]
I. Gohman, Vera Kennedy, 1922- ill. II. Moncure, Jane Belk. My "i" sound box. III. Title.
IV. Series: Moncure, Jane Belk. My first steps to reading.
PZ7.M739Myi 1984b [E] 84-17542
ISBN 0-89565-274-9

Distributed by Childrens Press, 1224 West Van Buren Street, Chicago, Illinois 60607.

© 1984 The Child's World, Inc.
All rights reserved. Printed in U.S.A.
Special Revised Edition.

My "i" Book

(This book concentrates on the short "i" sound in the story line. Words beginning with the long "i" sound are included at the end of the book.)

Little
had a
box.

"I will fill my box," she said.
Little went skip, skip,
skip up a hill.

She found inchworms,

lots of little
inchworms.

The inchworms wiggled and wiggled.

"What wiggly inchworms," she said.

She put the inchworms into her box.

Then Little i found iguanas, lots of iguanas.

The iguanas wiggled.

"What wiggly iguanas," she said.

She put the iguanas into the box with the inchworms.

The inchworms were not happy.

Out they jumped.

The iguanas jumped out too.

Away they went.

Little could not find the inchworms or

the
iguanas.

They were hiding.

Then Little

found an igloo.

She put the igloo into her box.

But the sun came out.
Guess what.
box
The igloo melted.

"Who will help me
fill my box?" she said.

An Indian came by.

"I will help you
fill your box," she said.

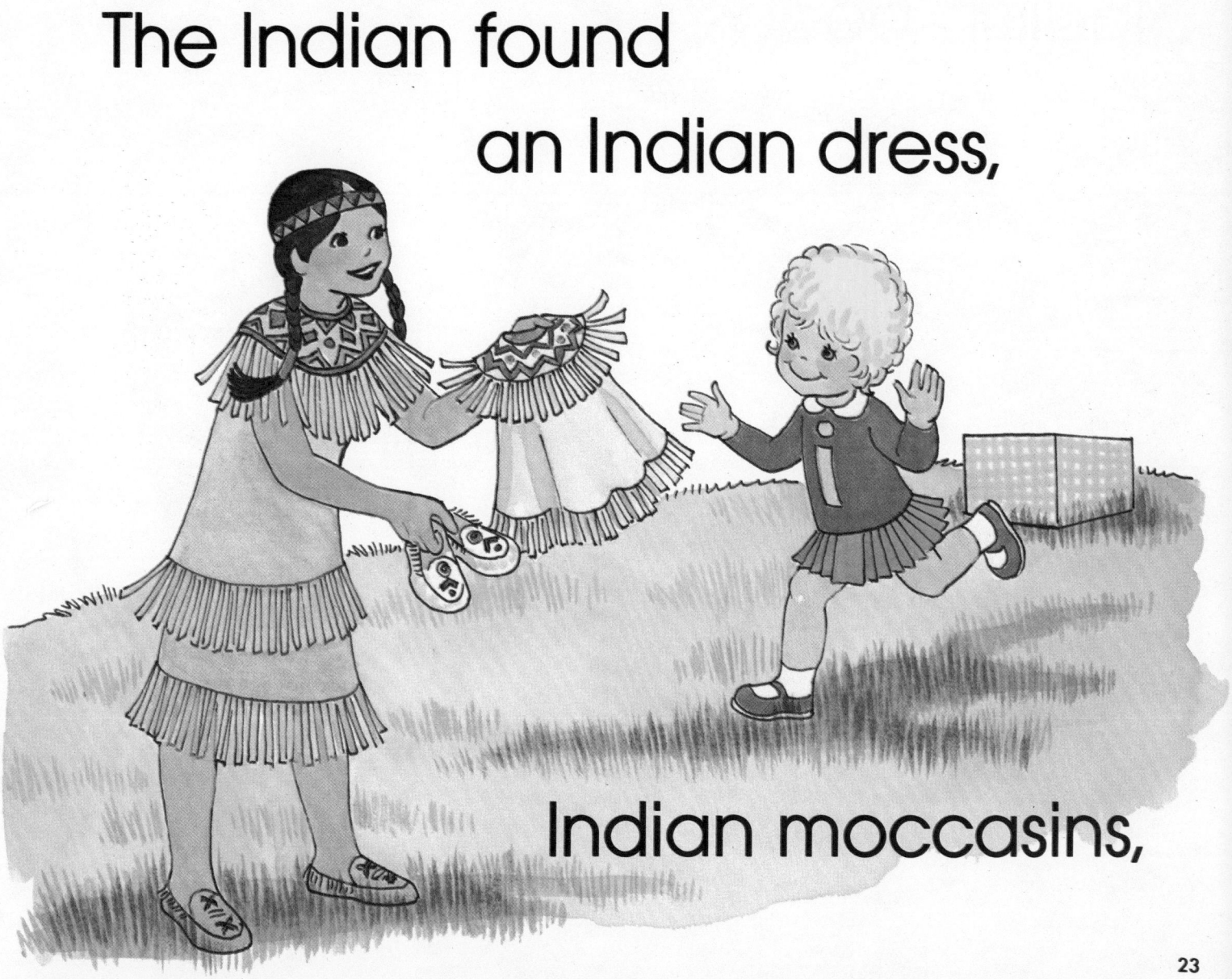
The Indian found
an Indian dress,
Indian moccasins,

Indian beads,

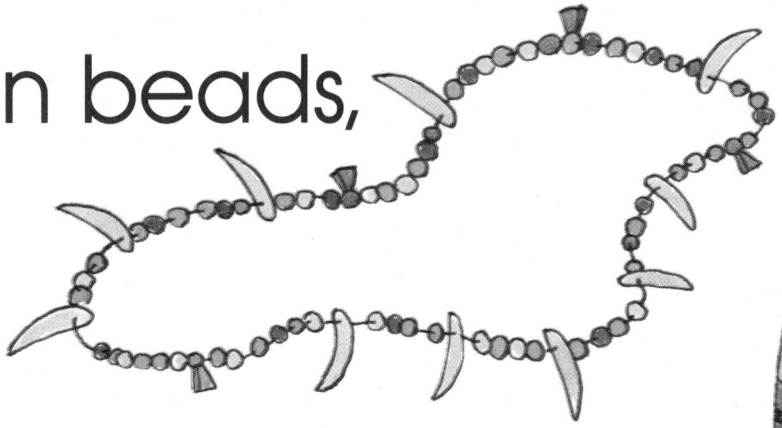

an Indian drum,

and an Indian headband.

Guess where they put
the Indian things.

"Thank you," said Little .

"Now I will dress like an Indian!"
And she did!
inchworms

Indian
iguana

More words with Little i.

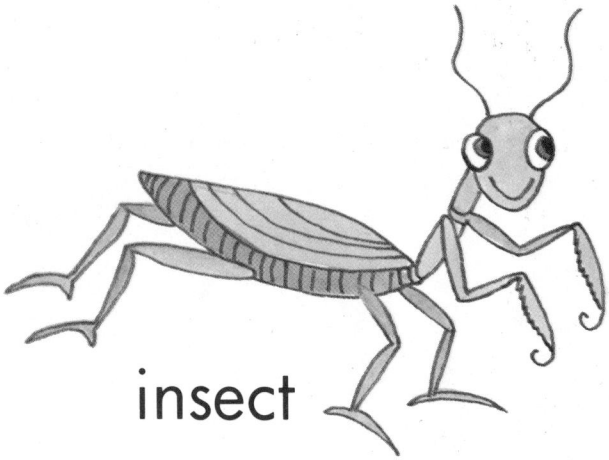

insect

ink

infant

imp
1
2
3
inch
Inga's
INN
inn

Little has another sound in some words.

She says her name.

Listen for Little 's name.

ice cubes

ice cream